D1454624

Weird Tales from the Storyteller

Daniel Morden

Illustrations by Jac Jones

PONT

First Impression—2003

ISBN 1 84323 210 3

© text: Daniel Morden
© illustrations: Jac Jones

Daniel Morden has asserted his right under the Copyright,
Designs and Patents Act, 1988, to be identified as Author of
this Work.

This book is published with the financial support of the
Welsh Books Council.

Printed in Wales at
Gomer Press, Llandysul, Ceredigion

To M and M and M.

Thanks to Robin Gwyndaf of the Museum of Welsh Life, who has collected many wonderful stories, including *Robin Ddu* from Lewis T. Evans of Clwyd.

CONTENTS

Daniel Morden, storyteller

Introduction: Welsh Whispers

I have always been a storyteller. When I was young, children could walk to school by themselves. Every day as I walked I would make up a story, about myself, or Spiderman, or the Viking God Thor, or some strange character I had invented. When I reached school, if I hadn't finished the story, I would walk around the playground, muttering it under my breath. I had to know how the story ended, even though I was making it up. The other children would see me riding imaginary horses or climbing imaginary castle walls.

Nowadays I visit schools to tell stories. I watch the children at playtime from the staffroom, and sometimes I see a boy or girl doing the same thing. Perhaps you know someone like that. Perhaps you are someone like that. If you are, I hope that we will meet one day and swap stories.

Have you ever played Chinese Whispers?

A group of people sit in a circle. Someone whispers a sentence to the person sitting beside him. She whispers what she has heard into the ear of the person beside her, and so on. The whisper travels around the circle and comes back to the ear of the one who first whispered it. But the whisper has changed during its journey! Sometimes there's nothing left of the original sentence.

The stories in this book don't belong to me. I'm just one of the whisperers. I don't know who started the game. I know that it began long ago, when birds would make their nests in old men's beards. I don't know if anything of the original whisper has survived. I do know that people don't remember boring stories. Hundreds, maybe thousands, of people have taken part in the game. Everyone who played tried to make the whisper exciting or memorable. So these stories have been made by many imaginations. If you like a story in this book then please tell it to someone else. You become part of a chain of Welsh whisperers that reaches back to the time of magic . . .

Robin Ddu and his Brothers

Once upon a time there lived three brothers. They were farmers.

The oldest two had bullied and stolen their way to a fortune. They had cows in the fields and sheep on the hills. They wanted for nothing, and yet they stomped around their land, spitting and cursing.

You see, their brother, Robin Ddu, was as sly as a fox. And try though they might, they couldn't get the better of him. Between their huge farms was a little strip of dusty ground. Robin lived there, in a tumble of a shack. It was only the ivy growing on the walls that was keeping the place upright. One cow he had, and she was a bag of bones.

You'd think his brothers would have contented themselves with gloating over their wealth, but no. The very thought of that thread of land had them grinding their teeth.

9

One night they had an idea. Next morning when Robin went out to milk the cow he found her lying dead. She'd been slaughtered during the night. She hadn't been much of a beast, but she'd meant the world to him. He went back into his shack and lit a candle and sat and thought.

When the candle was no more than a puddle of wax, he knew what to do. Next morning he skinned the cow.

On Robin's land there was a bony old crow that had broken its wing. Robin had tamed it so much it ate out of his hand. Every time he gave it a scrap it would utter a dry, 'Caark!' Robin took it onto his arm now, and set off for the town.

As Robin trudged to town the sky opened. The rain fell upon him in black sheets. He ran to the nearest house, the home of a Minister. He knocked and knocked until a young woman, the Minister's daughter, answered.

'What do you want?'

'Good morning. Is the Minister in? Or his wife?'

'No. Now, what do you want?'

'I wonder if you can help me. You see, I haven't slept a wink all night. I've forgotten The Lord's Prayer. Could you tell me how it begins?'

'Is that all? It begins with

"Our Father,

Who art in Heaven . . ."'

'Wait!' said Robin, 'are you saying that God is our father?'

'Yes, of course,' said the woman.

'Then that means you and I are brother and sister! You wouldn't leave your own brother out in the rain, would you?'

'My own brother? . . . I suppose not. You'd better come in . . . but not for long.'

In he went.

The house was full of the warm smell of stew.

'You wouldn't begrudge your own flesh and blood something to eat and something to drink, would you?'

She scowled. 'There's only bread and cheese.'

He ate and drank a little.

'Is there somewhere I could rest?'

'There's a heap of straw in the corner . . . but I want you gone by lunchtime!'

Robin lay down, closed his eyes and snored as if he was asleep.

There was a knock at the door.

'That'll be the Minister,' he thought. 'Now I'll get a decent feed.'

He watched her shoot an anxious look in his direction.

When she opened the door who came in but the miller's son, and didn't the two of them kiss and cuddle!

'Who's that?" said the miller's son.

'Never mind him, he's asleep. Look what I've made you!'

She opened the cupboard. There was the pot of stew.

'And this, too!'

She had him lift the hearthstone. There was a fine fruit-cake.

Just as they settled down to eat, there was a knock at the door.

'That's my father! If he finds you here he'll be furious! You must hide and I'll get rid of him.'

'Where?' said the miller's son.

'In the oven.'

He jumped in and she slammed the door.

She put the stew back in the cupboard, and the fruit-cake under the hearthstone. Then she opened the front door.

'There you are! Don't you know it's raining outside?'

'What are you doing back so early?'

'My horse lost a shoe. What's for lunch?'

'Just bread and cheese.'

'Well, that will have to do.'

He sat down. 'This bread is hard as a stone. Stoke up the fire under the oven. We'll bake some more.'

The poor girl did as she was bid.

The Minister saw Robin.

'Is that Robin Ddu?'

'It is. I'm waiting for the rain to pass.'

'What have you there?'

'A holy crow.'

'Whoever heard of such a thing?'

'It's true! God speaks through this bird. Give it a scrap to eat and it will speak.'

The Minister threw it a lump of stale bread.

'Cark!'

'What did it say?'

'It said God is pleased with your work and he has sent gifts of thanks. Open the cupboard and you'll see.'

The daughter ran to the cupboard.

'How did that get there!' she shouted. 'A miracle!'

'Goodness!' said the Minister. 'Perhaps there's something in it after all!'

They sat once more at the table and ate the stew.

'What's that tapping coming from the oven?' said the Minister.

'Oh,' said the young woman, 'it always does that as it warms up.'

'The crow said *gifts*. Are there any more besides the stew?'

'Cark!'

'It says to lift the hearthstone,' said Robin Ddu.

They found the cake.

'The Lord moves in mysterious ways!' marvelled the Minister.

'Amen to that!' said the daughter.

They ate the cake.

'Let us make it speak again.'

'I couldn't do that. It only speaks three times a day, and I need God to speak to me next, to tell me how I can make some money.'

'I tell you what. Why don't I pay you three gold coins to let the crow speak a third time?'

'Very well. Since you're the Minister.'

Robin trousered the gold.

'Cark!'

'Oh, my Heavens!' gasped Robin.

'What now?'

'The devil has burrowed up from Hell! He's waiting to jump out of the oven! It's him we've been hearing tapping!'

'Where's my Bible? Daughter! Stand behind me! Robin, open the door!'

Robin opened the oven. Out came a thick cloud of black smoke, and in the smoke the miller's son, screaming, his clothes on fire.

He knocked the Minister to the floor and was out of the house in a flash.

The Minister's daughter said, 'Father, did you see him?'

'It was too quick.'

'It was him!' she said. 'I wouldn't have believed it if I hadn't seen it with my own eyes. As soon as he saw your Bible, he was off.'

'Good gracious! Shut that oven door and put a rock against it! Robin, forgive me for doubting you.'

When the rain stopped, off went Robin to the market. But first he cut slits, like pockets, into the cowhide. Into each slit he slipped a golden coin.

Then he went on his way, with the hide on his back. He ambled into the nearest inn and hung the hide on a coat hook. He ordered a drink and a meal. The landlord gave him a look hard enough to bruise.

'Show me your money and I'll show you the meal.'

Robin took his crook and gave the cowhide a thwack. Out tumbled two golden coins.

'There you are,' said Robin.

The landlord gaped at the hide. He scratched his head.

'What is that about?'

'Oh, that? That's my magic cowhide. Every time I thwack it, money comes out.'

'How much d'you want for it?'

'Oh, I couldn't sell it. It's been in my family for generations.'

'Name your price!'

'Well, I'd need a bagful of gold.'

'Done!'

That night just as Robin's eldest brother was heading for the cowshed, who should walk by but Robin Ddu. And his pockets were jangling.

'I tell you what, you did me a very good turn indeed when you slaughtered my cow. I went into town with the hide and it seems cowhides are in great demand! Welsh cowhide hats are all the rage in London. Everyone's wearing them! I sold that hide for its weight in gold.' And he pulled a handful of gold coins from his pocket.

Robin's brother smiled with his mouth but not with his eyes. He nodded and said, 'That's wonderful!'

As soon as Robin was gone, he ran to the other brother and told him every word that Robin had said.

That night they slaughtered their herds: they killed every single cow.

Next morning they went into town.

'Cowhides here! Who'll buy our cowhides? The height of London fashion! Cowhides going cheap!'

'How much?' said the tanner.

'Their weight in gold!'

'How much!' said the tanner and walked away, shaking his head.

'Cowhides, cowhides, worth their weight in gold!' they cried.

Along came the innkeeper. 'Yesterday one of those rogues tricked me into buying a stinking, scrawny cowhide! Teach them a lesson, boys . . .'

Robin met his brothers on the road, bruised and battered and boiling with fury. Before he could open his mouth they grabbed him.

'Not another word! No more tricks from you! You're going for a swim in the sea and you're not coming back out!'

They stuffed him in a sack and set off.

It was a hot day, and on the way they came to an inn. What harm would there be in taking a drink? They dropped the sack outside and went in.

Robin sat in the sack and listened. He heard bleating. A shepherd was passing with his flock. The shepherd saw the sack moving.

'Maybe there's a pair of hens in there, or a cockerel,' he said to himself. 'Here's a chance to make some mischief.'

He gave the sack an almighty kick.

Robin shouted, 'Ow! Sorry, parson, you can kick me all you want. I won't go! No! I won't hear of it!'

'What are you doing in there? Won't hear of what?' said the shepherd.

'The parson wants me to go to Heaven. He's found a way to get there while we're still alive. It's something to do with a long ladder. He can't go, he's too busy what with all the sinners hereabouts. Someone has to, because St Peter has climbed all the way down and he's waiting. The parson wants me to go, but I won't because I'm enjoying myself so much down here. So the parson stuck me in this sack and he's lugging me to the ladder. I don't want to go! It's wonderful down here, with the

work, and the rain, and the wind, and the cold, and the
sickness, and the poverty –'

'Sorry about that kick I gave you!' said the shepherd. 'To
make up for it I'll go to Heaven instead of you. I'll open the
sack. You get out and I'll get in. What do you say?'

'I don't know . . .' said Robin. 'The parson specifically
said it should be me.'

'He'll never know! . . . I won't say a word. Take my sheep!'

So he opened the sack. Out came Robin and in went the shepherd and Robin went home with the sheep.

Robin's brothers came out of the tavern. They lugged the sack to a cliff and threw it off.

Splosh!

When they got back to the farm who should they see but Robin! With a flock of sheep!

'You did me a very good turn indeed when you threw me in the sea! You know that old story about a land under the waves? It's true! I got out of the sack, and there were fields and flocks of sheep everywhere! I brought back all the sheep I could, but there are flocks more down there.'

'Really?' said the brothers. 'Let's go and jump in the sea!' They ran all the way back to the cliff, fighting each other all the way, shouting:

'I was first!'

'I'm older than you!'

When they came to the water's edge they saw the reflection of the fluffy clouds in the sky and said, 'It's true! There they are!'

Splosh! Splosh!

They went in, but they didn't come out.

As for Robin Ddu, he had his brothers' farms now, too.

He lived happy,
So may we.
Put on the kettle,
We'll have a cup of tea!

Frosty

Once, six fools met.

The first fool was as white as milk. His skin was white. His eyes were white. His hair was white. His tongue was white. He wore a white hat over his white left ear. White mist curled from his lips and his nostrils. His knees knocked. His teeth chattered. He was the first fool.

As he walked he met the second. He had the ears of a donkey. He lay on his belly with one ear against the ground.

The first fool said, 'What is your name? And what are you doing?'

'Ssh! I'm listening to the speeches at the Houses of Parliament!'

'Ssh! is a funny name. Mine is Frosty. If you come with me we'll make our fortune!'

As the two fools walked they met a third. One side of her face was like your face or my face, but the other side was one enormous eye. She had a rifle. She put her eye to the sights and BANG!

'What did you shoot?' said Frosty.

'Across the sea in America there is a hill.

On that hill there is a wood.

In that wood there's a tree.

On that tree there's a branch.

On that branch there's a twig.

On that twig there's a leaf.

On that leaf there's a fly.

And I just shot out that fly's left eye.'

'What a shot! . . . Come with us and we'll make our fortune.'

'Of course!'

'I'm Frosty and this is Ssh!'

'I'm See Far.'

Off they went.

As the three fools walked they met a fourth. This fool, her cheeks were so baggy they dangled under her chin. She sucked in air. Her cheeks bulged and then she blew. The birds tumbled across the sky. The clouds scattered in every direction.

'What are you doing?' said Frosty.

'There's a windmill five miles away. I'm turning the sails.'

'Come with us! Together we'll make our fortune. I'm Frosty, this is Ssh! and See Far.'

'I'm Gusty.'

The four fools met a fifth. The fifth fool was hopping. He was hopping because he was holding one of his legs under his arm.

'Why have you taken off your leg?'

'I didn't want to go too fast.'

'Do you want to come with us? We're going to make our fortune.'

'Of course!'

'I'm Frosty, this is Ssh!, See Far and Gusty.'

'I'm Long Shanks.'

Off they went.

As the five fools walked, they met a sixth. He was a slip of a man, but he was carrying a tree over his shoulder.

'Who are you?' said Frosty.

'I'm the smallest giant in the world.'

'Come with us. We're off to make our fortune.'

'Of course!'

'I'm Frosty, this is Ssh!, See Far, Gusty and Long Shanks.'

'I am Small Tall.'

Off they went.

They came to a town where a soldier was blowing his horn, shouting:

'If anyone can outrun the princess, they will win as much gold as they can carry! But lose the race and you'll lose your head!'

'There's a chance to make our fortune!' said Frosty. He and his friends went straight to the palace.

The king looked at them, their eyes and ears and cheeks and hats . . . He smiled and his eyes glinted.

'Welcome! . . . You've come for the race! Fetch the princess!'

Out came the princess. Long Shanks screwed his leg

23

back on. See Far fired her gun and whoosh! The race began. They were gone in a flash.

'Ssh!,' said Frosty, 'is Long Shanks winning?'

Ssh! put his ear to the ground . . . 'The King has sent soldiers to roll barrels into Long Shanks's path! He's falling over again and again!'

'I have an idea!' said See Far.

BANG! See Far fired her rifle. The bullet knocked the barrel out of the path of Long Shanks and into the path of the princess. BANG! BANG! Again and again.

Zoom! Back came Long Shanks.

'Oh, well done! You have won the race,' said the King. 'But I'm afraid there is another task you must perform before you can have the gold. You see that lake? You must drain it dry by tomorrow. And if you don't, then I will cut off your heads.'

'I have an idea!' said Gusty.

That night Gusty blew so hard, all of the water in the lake was blasted into the sky. The lake became a cloud. The cloud flew to the other side of the world, and rained on a desert. The people there wept for joy.

When the King saw that the lake was dry he was amazed.

'Well! Well . . . well . . . done!' said the King. 'Tonight we shall have a feast!'

He led them to a room made all of metal, its walls shiny and its floor like a saucepan bottom.

Once the six fools were inside, the King slammed the door shut. Then he had his guards light a fire under the floor.

The floor glowed red hot. The walls glowed red hot.

The roof glowed red hot. The door glowed red hot. They were going to be baked to death!

Frosty smiled. He lifted his cap. Out of his ear came a blizzard! Ice dangled from the ceiling. Snow covered the floor.

The next morning, the King opened the door to find them cuddling together to stay warm! He was speechless.

'Your highness, you promised us as much gold as we could carry. No more tricks! Give us what we deserve!' commanded Frosty.

'Of course!' said the King. 'Guards!'

A sack was brought. The smallest giant in the world, Small Tall, took it and held it open. The guards tipped gold inside until it was full.

'I could carry another,' said Small Tall.

So they found another sack . . . and then another, and another, until Small Tall could no longer be seen.

'Another!' came his little voice from amongst the sacks.

Off they went, with six sacks of gold!

Once they had passed out of sight, the King said, 'Guards! Fetch the army! Tell them to kill those fools and bring me back my gold!'

Over the hill Ssh! had his ear to the ground.

'The army is coming! The King wants us dead!'

Countless as ants, the soldiers came, swarming towards the fools. Gusty blew. Hundreds of soldiers were blasted into the sky. Frosty lifted his hat. The rest were frozen to the spot.

See Far aimed her rifle and shot once. The King's crown toppled from his head!

The king was so terrified that he hid in the darkest of his dungeons, and he never troubled them again.

Frosty and his friends built a grand castle where they lived very happily.

I've been there and played the fiddle!

Them Ones

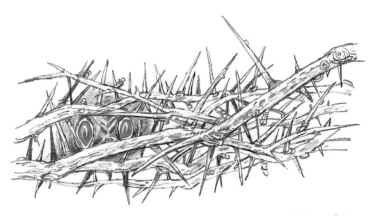

One Sunday Jac was sitting by the fire, picking his nose. Now and then, with a grunt, he would lean forward and peer out of the greasy little window of his clom cottage. What did he see? Mist and drizzle, and drizzle and mist. The fire would spit then, and Jac would sit back and give a little sigh of contentment. Sometimes he warmed the front of his hands, and sometimes the back of his hands. What with the front and the back of his hands to warm, it looked as though he was going to have a busy afternoon.

Mali stumbled in from the yard.

'Look at you! My layabout son! . . . Where did I go wrong? I'm wet through from feeding the pigs and the cows and digging the garden, and there you are cooking like a chicken in the oven! Get out! Get out and don't come back until you've a fish for our supper! And not a tiddler, mind you. I want something worth eating!'

'But it's raining!'

'Good! You could do with a wash. The river will be good and murky and the fish will be easy to catch. I won't settle for anything less than a trout or a salmon.'

She grabbed him by the scruff of the neck and pushed him out of the door.

Jac opened his mouth to speak but his coat landed on his head.

He pulled it off, opened his mouth, but his cap slapped against his face.

He opened his mouth for a third time and the door slammed.

'Is there anything worse than my mother?' he muttered to himself.

Jac pulled on his coat and his cap, fetched his coracle and rod and off he went. The fine drizzle settled on him without fuss. At first he was bejewelled, then he was sodden, then stiff with cold. He tried not to think about the fire. For the first time he felt a certain sympathy for the stupid sheep.

The river was as brown as chocolate. Jac didn't notice the woodpecker, the kingfisher and the tree creeper. He was too busy kicking stones. He found a slimy spot on the bank to slide in the coracle . . .

But a flash of something in the meadow caught his eye. Something low and brown, moving through the long grass. What could it be? Jac thought he knew. A river cat. The scourge of the fisherman. A romping otter. What else could it possibly be?

And it was in the meadow. There was a good chance Jac would catch him before he melted into the river. He could be home for tea within the hour! His mother would be overjoyed. A long, fine otter pelt would fetch a pretty penny. Jac dropped the coracle and rod and ran. There was that flash of brown again! What was it doing so far from the water?

'High and dry he is!' Jac chuckled as he ran.

It ducked into a gap among the roots of an ancient oak.

Jac picked up a stone and stuffed it into the gap between the tree-roots. Something inside was scratching and scuffing the stone. He ran around the tree and found another gap on the opposite side. He took off his coat and stretched it over the hole.

Thump. Something ran headlong into his coat.

He wrapped it around the thing. Jac could not believe his good fortune! Already he was practising the fib he would tell his mother when he gave her only half of the price of the pelt.

But the squirming thing in his arms wasn't crouching, It was standing. Jac gripped it tightly with one arm, then with the other he uncovered the top of it . . .

Something ancient stared back, with the face of an aged child. It was as white and round and cold as the moon. Jac was so close he tasted its breath on his tongue, the stink of rotting carrion.

'My mother is calling. Must she come and fetch me?'

Jac had thought himself cold from the rain before, but now he was cold in another way. He shuffled back from his coat, shivering.

The thing stared at him without blinking. Jac returned the gaze for a moment and then looked away. Compared to this thing, Jac was a mayfly, a drift of mist from the lips on a winter's morning.

'Would you like my mother's blessing?'

'NO! . . . no. No need for your mother's blessing, your honour. You go on now, and I'll be heading off. Good day, and sorry to have troubled you.'

Jac turned his back on it, and half-walked, half-ran back to the farm.

As Mali opened the door she was about to shout when she saw the expression on Jac's face.

'What is the matter?'

Jac went past her without a word, to the back of the farmyard.

'Where's your coat? And the coracle?'

He broke off the branches from the hawthorn tree frantically, until he'd pricked his hands red and torn his shirt-sleeves to rags.

When she saw what her son was about, and the urgency with which he was about it, the colour drained from his mother's face too. She fetched her gloves and helped him. Together they wove the broken branches into a filigree that surrounded the cottage.

Once they had done so, they stepped over their defences and into the house.

'I'm sorry,' he said, 'there's nothing for our tea. I'd rather have your curse than that other mother's blessing.'

And for once his mother didn't argue. For she knew better than to bring upon herself the anger of The Fair Folk. The Mother's Blessing. The Good People.

Them Ones.

The Bwca

An old farmer and his wife lived on a hill out of town. They had never been blessed with children, and as the years went by, it became harder by the day to do the heavy work. At last they resolved to take on a lad to work for them, and so they walked into town on market-day. There was a place people would stand if they needed a job. Sure enough, among the crowd there was a young man. His name was Owen.

They fetched him back to the farm. Within the week they wondered how they'd ever managed without him. He wasn't a talkative boy, but he got on with his tasks without complaint. He could turn his hand to anything.

So when the snow began to fall one winter's morning, Owen said he would go and see if the sheep on the hill were safe, and had shelter and food.

He put on his hat, and his gloves, and his scarf, and his coat, and his boots, and went out into the white world. He had to push hard against the kitchen door to open it. The snow was gathering in drifts.

The farmer and his wife sat by the fire and waited for him to return. They sat by the fire all night.

Next morning they put on their hats, and their gloves, and their scarves, and their coats, and their boots, and went to look for him.

They found his body. He'd become lost in the woods, and rather than blunder in the dark, he'd lain down, shivering.

Until the shivering had stopped.

The old man and the old woman were heart-broken. It was as though they'd lost a son of their own. They loaded his body on a wagon and took it down through the icy lanes to the town. They buried him in the ground.

The night after the funeral the old man was woken by his wife.

'What's the matter?'

'Listen!' she hissed.

There was a scritching, scratching, scraping sound coming from outside. From the farmyard. They lay awake all night, too afraid to go to the window to see what was making the noise.

When the morning came they shuffled over to the kitchen door and leaned against it – they were expecting to have to push against a drift – but the door swung open easily.

The whole farmyard had been cleared of snow. The sound they'd heard the night before had been the sound of shovelling. The snow was piled in a heap at one end of the yard. They were bewildered. Who had done this?

Next night they lay awake to the sound of hammering.

Next morning they got up to find all the holes in the roof of the barn had been mended. The night after that, a fence was built around the farmyard, a fence they'd always wanted, but had never had the money nor the time to build.

On that third day they went down into town to see the Cunning Man. They told him what had happened. He listened, sucking his gums. At last, he said:

'You know the wood behind your farmhouse? When I was small I saw a Bwca there. I reckon it's him that's helping you.'

'Bwca?' they said. 'What's a Bwca?'

'A spirit. They can take whatever form they wish, but their true form is something like a child, and something like an old man. Scrawny and hairy they are, with a snout of a nose and prick ears. People say the Bwca was old when God was a boy. If he likes you he'll help you, but if he doesn't like you he'll make your life a misery.'

'Why does he like us?' said the old woman.

'I reckon he feels sorry for you. He probably watched Owen die in his wood. He's making up for the loss of Owen.'

The old woman thought, this Bwca, if he's helping us, we should reward him.

So that night she poured some of the cream, the top of the milk, into a bowl. She opened the kitchen door, walked out across the farmyard and into the barn. She put the bowl down in front of the haystack.

She stood still a moment. She whispered into the dark, 'Bwca – thank you for what you've done for us.'

36

Something shuffled in the shadows.

The old woman bolted across the yard, into the kitchen, slammed the kitchen door and sat by the fire. Even though she could feel the heat of the flames, she shivered.

Next morning they got up – and found the animals fed and watered, the tools sharpened, the cows milked.

And the bowl licked clean.

It was that way from then on. Every night they'd put out a bowl of cream. Every night the Bwca would work on their behalf. The sound of him would lull them to sleep.

In the spring he'd plough the fields and sow the seeds.

In the summer he'd shear the wool from the sheep.

In the autumn he'd harvest the crops.

In the winter he'd make sure the sheep and cows and pigs were safe and warm.

The animals were never sick. The cows gave the best milk in the region. If you went to the farmhouse you'd find legs of meat hanging from the rafters, ready to sell at market. You'd find lumps of cheese, and butter, and churns full of creamy milk.

One night an old friend arrived with good news. Her daughter had just given birth to a baby girl. As they sat by the fire, the friend described the child.

'Her hands are as white and delicate as any I've ever seen.'

From the darkness above them came a cracked voice, 'The Bwca's hands are whiter still.'

Into the light came a pale, three-fingered hand. The twig-like fingers curled into the palm and the hand slipped back into the shadows.

All that year the old man and his wife were happy. Their pockets jangled. For the first time in their lives they had money to spare. So they resolved to take on a maid. On market-day they walked down into town and went to the place where people would stand if they needed a job. There was a young woman. Pretty thing she was.

Her name was Eirwen.

They fetched her back to the farm, and the very first task they gave her to do was to take the bowl of cream to the barn.

'It's for the Bwca,' they said.

She stepped out of the kitchen. She heard the door close behind her. No one to see. The wind blew around her skirts. She stood in the yard in the gathering dark.

She thought for a moment, then muttered scornfully to herself, 'Bwca! . . . No such thing. That's just a story.'

She lifted the bowl to her lips and drank the cream. Then she scooped up some water from a puddle, walked into the barn and put down the bowl.

'Bwca . . . Thank you for what you've done for us!' she smirked, and skipped back to the kitchen.

That night the old woman woke up her husband.

'What's the matter?'

'Listen!'

'I can't hear anything! You woke me up for nothing!'

'Neither can I! That's what I mean . . . Where's the Bwca? Every other night we can hear him!'

They lit a rushlight and shuffled over to where the maid was sleeping. They shook her shoulders and woke her up.

'Did you put the bowl of cream out like we told you to for the Bwca?'

The maid looked up at the two of them, looming over her, the rushlight making wild shadows on their faces. She was afraid suddenly. The sleep had left her muddled, and she wanted to keep her job.

'Of course!' she said, and rolled over and pressed her face against the pillow.

Next morning they prowled the farm. No sign that the Bwca had been busy . . . except in the barn they found his cream bowl smashed into shards.

For a week there was silence.

Then the Bwca returned.

They found themselves remembering what the Cunning Man had said: if the Bwca liked you he'd help you. If he didn't like you, he'd make your life a misery.

Whatever they did by day now, the Bwca would undo at night.

If they dug a hole he'd fill it in.

If they built a wall he'd tear it down.

If they ploughed a field he'd make the grass grow high overnight.

In the spring he'd tear open their sacks of seed and scatter them in the river.

In the summer the sheep died one by one.

In the autumn he snapped the ploughs and hobbled the horses.

In the winter he tore holes in the roof of the barn and hid the tools.

They couldn't keep the farm-hands. Their livelihood was in ruins.

One night, as the household slept, invisible hands grabbed the maid by the hair, dragged her down the stairs and out through the front door. The Bwca threw her over the farmhouse, ran around it and caught her.

Again he threw her and caught her. The third time she landed in the duckpond. Bruised, shivering, she went back to bed. Next morning when she woke up, she saw a bucket swinging over her head! She found herself lying on a thin plank stretched across the well. She screamed for help, screamed and screamed. Once she was off that plank, she fled without another word.

Desperate to end this nightmare, the old people sent for the Minister to pray the Bwca away. They were so relieved to see him. The old man took the Minister's horse, gave it hay and water, while his wife led him inside.

The Minister knelt in front of the fire, his elbows on a stool, murmuring to himself. Suddenly the stool was yanked away, the minister's face hit the flagstone floor, and blood burst from his nose. He sat up . . . and saw the impossible. It was as though a living mirror was before him. An exact twin of himself stood over the Minister, even down to the Bible, grinning from ear to ear.

The old man and his wife watched the Minister run screaming from the farmhouse, leap onto his horse and bolt from the yard. Nothing would coax him to return.

One night the farmer and his wife were in bed when they heard the kitchen door open. The Bwca was in the kitchen. Such a commotion! Next morning they opened the door. What a sight! Pots and pans everywhere, broken crockery, doors torn off their hinges, windows smashed. The legs of meat hanging from the rafters were writhing

with flies. The cheese and the butter were covered in a fur of mould. The milk in the churns was orange and sour.

The old man turned to his wife.

'This place is blighted,' he said. 'No good will come of it again. We must leave before the Bwca ruins us.'

So they loaded a few things on the back of their wagon – a cauldron, some blankets, a few tools, the spinning wheel – and set off.

As they headed down the hill one of their neighbours met them.

'Where are you going?' he asked.

'Anywhere,' said the farmer. 'Anywhere is better than here. We'll start again somewhere else.'

'Goodbye,' said the neighbour.

The wagon went by.

'Goodbye,' said the farmer over his shoulder.

The neighbour watched the wagon roll down the hill. Out of the cauldron popped a shaggy thing with a snout of a nose and prick-ears. It waved a paw and mouthed, 'Goodbye!'

King Herla

Long before the Angles and Saxons conquered the island of Britain, it was ruled over by many kings. Each King would have his own court. One such court was on a hill in a gentle, green region where England and Wales meet. And the absolute monarch of this region was King Herla.

One day King Herla heard from the courtyard of his castle a great commotion: when he went to his throne room, there was brought before him the strangest sight he had ever seen.

A dwarf rode into the throne room on the back of a goat. The dwarf was the size of a child, but it had the body of a man, and a bulbous head.

The face was old, so old, and fierce red, and covered in warts. His hair, his beard, were more like the red bristles of a pig. He wore a garment made of dappled doeskin, and at the bottom of his legs were not feet, but hooves.

Under his arm, the dwarf carried a little white dog. The dog jumped down and scampered about, barking. The dwarf smiled – one of those smiles that looked as much like a sneer.

The dwarf dismounted from the goat, bowed very low and said, 'I have come from far and not far. I am King of many lords and chiefs and a race beyond counting. I have come to make a pact with you.'

'What sort of a pact?' asked King Herla.

'Your highness,' said the Dwarf, 'months ago you sent a messenger to try to persuade the King of France to let you marry his daughter. Later today your messenger will at last return and announce that a match has been made. All I ask is that, as we are both kings, equals, I may serve you at your wedding feast and a year later you will serve me at mine.'

Now King Herla had indeed sent a messenger to France but it had been in secret and he had heard nothing from the messenger. Now this stranger knew his thoughts.

The king's court was silent and still except for the yapping dog. The King, as though in a dream, agreed to the dwarf's proposal. 'It shall be so,' he said.

As quick as thought, the dwarf was back on the goat, the dog jumped up and they were gone.

Before the King could say or do anything, there was another commotion from the courtyard and his messenger entered, announcing that his efforts had been successful – Herla *would* marry the daughter of the King of France.

On the wedding-day, at the time of the feast, as Herla

and his new wife sat at the High Table, there was suddenly amongst them a little white dog, running amongst the guests, yapping. Then there came a host of dwarves, with red faces and hairy arms, and outside there was a host of pygmy pavilions. From the pavilions came servants bringing food on great silver platters and fine wine in jugs of strange and delicate design. The food, the wine, tasted like nothing the king and his courtiers had ever tasted before. It was not to everyone's taste: some found it too strong.

The dwarves used nothing from Herla's kitchen. Everything Herla's cooks had prepared was left untouched. Wherever service was needed, the dwarves appeared as if they knew the guests' wishes even before the guests themselves knew them.

Another chair was set at the High Table and suddenly there he was, the Dwarf King, with his coarse features and red bristles, climbing up onto the chair, surveying the feast.

He turned to Herla and said, 'Best of Kings, as I have promised, I have come. If there is anything that you want I will supply it. If not, I ask that you honour your side of our bargain and be ready exactly a year from now to come to my land and wait upon me at my wedding.'

Without waiting for an answer, he returned to his pavilion and in the time it takes to blink an eye, the entire company, tents, dog and all, were gone.

So for a year, Herla lived with his new wife, pondering the agreement he'd made. And the people who'd been at that wedding found themselves craving the strange taste of the food and the wine. Then the year was up,

and there was a messenger, a red-faced dwarf on a goat, carrying stiffly under his arm the little white dog. So Herla and twenty trusted men followed the dwarf to the edge of Herla's gentle kingdom, where the land became rockier, more mountainous.

They crossed a brook and approached a cave in the side of a sheer cliff.

The dwarf nodded at the cave. He rode in on the goat.

As they followed him in, Herla and his men could see nothing. Utter blackness. And there was no sound. No hooves clopping, no breathing or coughing, nothing. Then Herla and his men saw a speck of red light. Then it was as big as a fist. Then a man's head. Then as big as a man. Then they were in the red light; it burst upon them like a wave. It came from everywhere. They were in a huge hall, so enormous that Herla couldn't see its end. A vault. Thick pillars rose up into the dark above them. There were steaming pools at their feet. The air was bitter and acrid. Many tables, covered in linen, were laid ready for a feast.

So Herla and his men did as they had promised. Throughout the wedding feast they waited on the little tables of the Dwarf King. They brought him and his guests food on ornate little plates, and wine in beautiful little goblets.

When it was over, the Dwarf King and his retinue climbed onto their goats, and Herla and his men onto their horses, and the dwarves led them from the vault into the dark and out of the dark, until they tasted fresh air on their tongues, and saw daylight, and felt wind on their faces. In the half-light of the cave the Dwarf King gave Herla gifts – crystals, and diamonds, and other bright stones.

He clicked his warty fingers and there was the little white dog. It jumped into Herla's arms.

'Goodbye, King Herla,' said the dwarf. 'Remember one thing. You must not dismount until the dog jumps to the ground.'

The Dwarf King and his companions turned back into the dark and were gone.

So Herla and his men galloped from the cave. It was evening. Everything looked different. There were more houses, and the river was deeper, broader. They saw a cottage of strange design. Herla approached it. A young man, dressed in strange clothes, emerged. He looked up, frowned and took off his hat.

Herla said, 'What news of my Queen?'

Hastily the man bowed. 'Who is your Queen? Where do you rule?'

'Why here!' said Herla. 'I am your king.'

The man said, 'But our king is Edmund.' He turned and called to his old grandmother. She came out and he told her what Herla had said.

'Herla . . . when I was little, there were legends of a King Herla – but he was lost in a cave, some two hundred years ago.'

Herla saw one of his men go to dismount . . . he thought of the dog and tried to speak but it was too late. Before Herla could utter a word, his man's foot touched the ground and twisted under him. There was a crack like the snap of a dry branch, the bones of his toes tumbled out of the ancient remains of the shoe and as he fell, his clothes, his skin, flaked into dust and fluttered away. His white bones broke through the grey, dry skin, his jaw fell from his skull, his eyes shrank back until the sockets were hollow, and a heap of bones fell with a clatter before them.

Two hundred years had elapsed during the day that they had been in the cave.

Somehow King Herla and the other riders found their way to the hill of the court – but there was only a green tump where his castle and grand hall had stood.

And ever since then, Herla and his men have been seen – sometimes by innocent minds in the still of the day, more often by travellers at night. And always, King Herla is riding without rest, through the Marches, waiting for the moment to come when the dog chooses to jump from his arms to the ground.

The Magic Well

Once upon a time, there was an ordinary girl. She wasn't beautiful, or clever, but she was good. She lived with her father. Her mother was dead. One day her father looked at her and said to himself, 'My daughter is growing into a young woman. What do I know about young women? She needs a mother. For her sake I must marry again.'

And so he found a beautiful young widow who had a lovely daughter of her own. She will make a fine wife and stepmother, he thought.

Soon there was a wedding. So the girl had a beautiful stepmother and a lovely stepsister.

The girl didn't mind that they were prettier than her. She had a new family! When she was alone with them she said to her stepsister, 'Come and see the hens and the cockerel!'

'What?' said the stepsister. 'And spoil my dress?'

And her stepmother said, 'I'm sorry, my dear, but we aren't interested in chickens or ducks or pigs or cows . . . They're dirty and they smell. You will look after them while we look after ourselves. Is that clear?'

The girl soon discovered they were as ugly on the inside as they were lovely on the outside. Whenever the father was out of sight, the stepmother gave her more and more errands. She had to cook, and wash, and sew, and spin until her back ached and her hands were sore. Whenever her father was near, they were telling lies about her, poisoning him against her.

The wife told him, 'I'm afraid you neglected her at just the wrong moment. She has become selfish, and wilful, and cruel. Hard work is the only remedy.'

It was as though the girl was a servant in her own house.

Because the father was kind and trusting, he believed his wife.

One hot summer's evening, while the father was away, the stepmother said, 'My dear, I want you to go to fetch water from the well in the forest.'

'But my father told me never to go to the well in the forest. He said strange creatures live there. Can't I get some water from the spring?'

'Tut, tut! A big girl like you, frightened of a few trees? They say the water from that well can make a girl blossom into beauty. I've heard that the prince has taken a mind to marry. Once my daughter has tasted that water, the prince will surely have her for his wife. Here's a bag full of food. Off you go, and don't come back until you have what I want!'

Before the girl could argue, she was bundled out of the door.

'Can I have a bucket?'

SLAM!

She looked in the bag. She found a few crusts of bread and a lump of hard cheese.

The girl looked around and shivered. The light was thickening. She swung the bag onto her shoulder and off she went, following the path into the forest. The trees frowned over her. The brambles tore at her sleeves. Dark things scuttled across the path.

Then, ahead, she saw a shape on a stone . . . when she came closer, she saw that it was a ragged old man. He lifted his head very slowly and smiled a smile so wide that the two ends of it nearly met at the back.

'Where are you going?' he asked her, kindly.

'I'm looking for the well.'

'What's in the sack?'

'Food. Are you hungry? There isn't much but you're welcome to share what I have.'

She gave him half of the bread and cheese. They ate in silence.

'You've been kind to me. I'll be kind to you. Take this.' He gave her a bottle with a cork. 'Soon you'll come to a hedge. You won't get through unless you sing:

> Hedge, hedge,
> Give me a hole.

'When you have done so, you'll find a well. Sit on the edge of the well and look inside. Don't be afraid. Don't be frightened by what you see.'

She bowed and said, 'Thank you,' and walked on.

She found herself at a thick hedge. She sang, as he told her to do:

> 'Hedge, hedge,
> Give me a hole.'

As soon as she had sung those words, the plants parted themselves that she might pass.

She had stepped through. And there on the other side was the well. She sat on the edge of the well and looked in. There was the reflection of the moon, quivering, and three heads bobbing in the water. Bobbing and rolling, the heads of three old men, with yellow-white skin like the belly of a dead fish. The eyes were closed and the mouths were open.

They opened their eyes and gazed at her and smiled. She tried to smile back.

They sang:

> 'Wash us, comb us,
> Set us down softly,
> Lay us on the bank to dry.'

The girl leaned into the well. She put one hand under the chin, and the other hand into the hair and lifted out the first head. It was slimy to the touch. Its hair was matted with twigs and weeds. Little squirming things wriggled from the beard.

Carefully, by moonlight, she combed the hair and the beard. She picked out the weeds and twigs, one by one. She did the same for the second and the third head.

When she'd finished, the heads turned to each other.

'What should we do for her?' one asked the other.

'Make her smell as sweet as summer,' was the answer.

By the time she had finished, the morning had come. The girl put the heads back into the well.

'Goodbye.'

She filled her bottle full of bright water and set off. Wherever she walked, flowers grew and birds sang. New blossoms appeared in the hedges and on the paths, like stars in the gloom.

Suddenly she stopped. She could hear a horse approaching. Can you guess who it was? The prince was hunting in the woods. He smelled a smell as sweet as the blossom of summer. He followed it until he found the girl . . . as soon as he saw her he fell in love with her, and she with him. Such joy! Such happiness! The prince and bride were married in the town and there were great celebrations.

Of course she invited her father, her stepmother and her stepsister. The father wept for joy. The stepmother and stepsister ground their teeth with fury.

'She wasn't as stupid as she looked,' said her step-sister bitterly. 'Mother, give me some food, I'm going into the woods where *she* went. I want to be a princess too!'

So, that very evening, she made herself ready. Sweet cakes and fruit she had in her bag. She swung it over her shoulder and off she went, following the path into the forest.

The light thickened. The trees frowned over her. The brambles tore at her sleeves. Dark things scuttled across the path.

Then, ahead, she saw a shape on a stone . . . when she came closer she saw that it was a ragged old man. He lifted his head very slowly and smiled a smile so wide that the two ends of it nearly met at the back.

He said, kindly, 'Where are you going?'

'What's that to you?'

'What's in the bag?'

'None of your business!'

The old man turned away. The stepsister walked on, laughing to herself.

Her way was soon blocked by a hedge. It was too long to walk around.

She tried to push her way through. It ripped her fine dress to rags, it tore out her lovely hair, it scratched her soft face until she bled.

Finally she burst out on the other side. She saw a well. She looked in. Ugh! She saw three heads bobbing and rolling, staring back at her. She screamed.

They sang –

'Wash us, comb us,
Set us down softly,
Lay us on the bank to dry'

The stepsister shouted, 'Heads! In the well!' She took a stone and Smack! Smack! Smack! She hit them, all three. They frowned.

'What should we do for her?' one of them asked.

'Make her smell as sour as sweat,' declared another.

She leaned over and scooped a handful of water. The water was foul and brackish and brown.

'Think of the prince!' she said to herself, and drank. Thick clouds of flies settled on her. She wailed and flailed her arms hopelessly. She ran for home, back through the hedge that tore her and scratched her, and back down the path. As she ran, the flowers in her footsteps wilted. The trees she passed wept their leaves.

She came to a town. What a sight she was! The hedge had torn her hair from her head in clumps, her face was scarred with scratches, her dress was filthy and frayed. She smelt so strong with sweat that passers-by pelted her with stones.

At last she came to her home.

'Mother!'

'You are not my daughter! My daughter is beautiful! I don't know you. Be off before I set the dog on you!'

She turned, and ran and ran, and cried and cried . . . until she heard a carriage approaching.

Can you guess who was inside?

The girl and the prince.

Can you guess what the girl had in her hand?

The bottle of bright water.

And what do you think she did? She was good, and kind. She gave it to her stepsister to drink.

And suddenly her stepsister was lovely again.

But this time she was lovely outside and in.

Dylan – Child of the Waves

Once upon a time in Gwynedd, there lived two magicians, husband and wife. The spells of Gwydion were feared the length and breadth of Wales. Beautiful Arianrhod enchanted everyone who met her. Each was jealous of the other's power.

They bickered and argued; they taunted each other with boasts and threats at every opportunity. Eventually they could no longer live together.

She built a shimmering palace that rose from the sea. At night, passers-by who looked at it were sure that they stared at the stars.

He built a sheer fortress on a hill. It frowned over the valleys below.

They would have battles of magic, each creating wonderful illusions to deceive and frighten the other.

One time, the husband sent a message to his wife.

"Your every move is watched by my servants. Your past and your future belong to me."

She sent a message back–

"You can no more control me than you can control the sea!"

"Come to my fortress, and I will show everyone, once and for all, which of us is the more powerful."

And so, one night, she left her shining tower, crossed the restless waves, and travelled to that fierce fortress. The gates of the stockade were opened before her. She walked through the courtyard. There was a great commotion from inside the hall: music, and song, and drunken laughter.

The hall doors parted. Kings and Queens, lords and ladies, musicians, poets and servants all turned to her. Suddenly the hall was still and silent.

In the centre of that great hall stood her husband. He held in his hand a strange wand. He knelt and held it out.

"Step over this," he said, "and the world will know you have no secrets from me."

What could she do? She was trapped. It was too late to refuse.

She lifted her dress and stepped carefully over the wand.

As soon as she did so, out from under her skirts – out from inside her – tumbled two strange somethings. Strange boy-children.

Her husband lunged forward and grabbed a child. The other one – a golden-haired boy – looked up . . . a hundred heads loomed over him, gasping, cursing, screaming.

He stretched out his hands towards his mother. She was shouting at his father. He reached to his father, but his father was laughing and taunting his mother.

He looked around again. He was a thing of shame. His arrival had been greeted with horror and anger.

He saw the open doors of the hall and he fled. He bolted through the thicket of legs, dodging the outstretched hands and snapping dogs, into the courtyard, scattering chickens and goats, slipping in the mud, over the wooden stockade wall, tumbling over and over down the hill, across the fields, until he was stumbling on stones . . . There before him was the sea. He remembered the silence of water when he was inside his mother. He waded into the shallows – the cold of it made him gasp – and he was gone into the depths.

And so he took to the waves. He was called Dylan Ail Ton – Son of the Ocean.

He built a palace beneath the waves, from wrecked ships and drowned cities.

The walls were studded with barnacles. Gaping eels and shimmering shoals passed through the open windows and doorways.

There he hoarded the things that had been lost at sea. He gathered mermaid's purse, white bones and shiny shells, sailor's love-letters, and starfish, and the crown of the king of the lowland hundreds, and the bells of drowned churches.

He danced to the songs of whales.

He chased dolphins between the wrecks and ruins.

His lullaby was the hiss and drag of the sea on shingle.

Sometimes, when a shaft of sunlight shone on the sea, his palace would be seen by fishermen.

On land they prayed to God, but at sea they prayed to Dylan.

The brightest of their catch they'd throw back over the side for him.

In return, he'd try to calm the angry waves, and guide them through the treacherous reefs. Sometimes a boy's head would be glimpsed among the watching seals, his eyes as black as wet pebbles. Sometimes he'd be seen squatting on a rock among the cormorants, stretching out his arms as though he too was drying his wings. His yellow hair went white as foam. He plaited it with bladderwrack.

His mother would sing to him from her tower.

His father would walk the beach and call to him.

But he never went to them.

He was neither his mother's nor his father's.

The rock where he sunned himself can still be seen even today. Long after his mother's palace and his father's fortress have crumbled to ruin.

It is called Maen Dylan.